愛麗絲夢遊仙境

Alice's Adventures in Wonderland,

原　著 *Lewis Carroll.*

改　編 **Anne Suzane**

Alice's Adventures in Wonderland,

Contents
目　　錄

愛麗絲發現一隻白兔子並且
發現一個新世界
ALICE FINDS A WHITE RABBIT
AND DISCOVERS A NEW WORLD
——— 1 ———

愛麗絲吃了一些蛋糕並且
改變大小
ALICE EATS SOME CAKE AND
CHANGES SIZE
——— 9 ———

愛麗絲和動物們比賽
ALICE AND THE ANIMALS
PLAY GAMES
——— 15 ———

愛麗絲發現白兔子的家
ALICE FINDS THE WHITE
RABBIT'S HOUSE
——— 21 ———

毛毛蟲
THE CATERPILLAR
——— 29 ———

愛麗絲夢遊仙境

愛麗絲遇見女伯爵和赤郡貓
ALICE MEETS THE DUCHESS AND THE CHESHIRE CAT
37

瘋狂賣帽子人的茶會
THE MAD HATTER'S TEA PARTY
47

皇后的花園
THE QUEEN'S GARDEN
57

愛麗絲打槌球並且碰到假烏龜
ALICE PLAYS CROQUET AND MEETS THE MOCK TURTLE
73

審問
THE TRIAL
81

愛麗絲捲入騙子的審問中
ALICE BECOMES INVOLVED IN THE TRIAL OF THE KNAVE
87

Alice's Adventures in Wonderland,

ALICE FINDS A WHITE RABBIT AND DISCOVERS A NEW WORLD

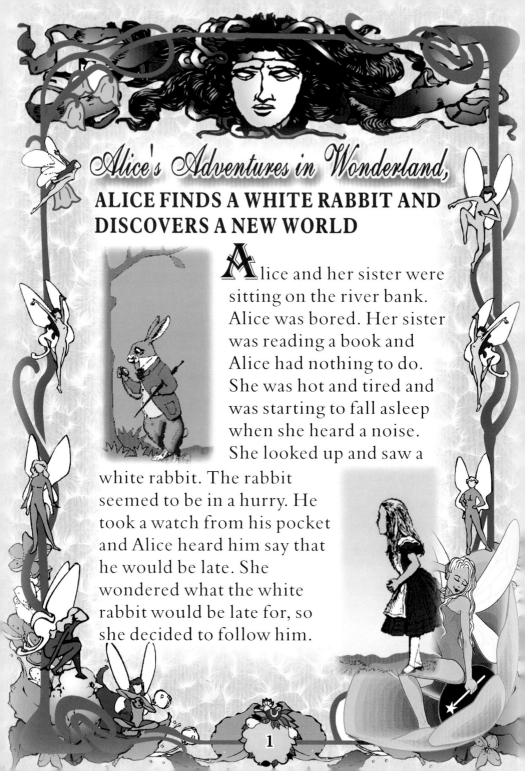

Alice and her sister were sitting on the river bank. Alice was bored. Her sister was reading a book and Alice had nothing to do. She was hot and tired and was starting to fall asleep when she heard a noise. She looked up and saw a white rabbit. The rabbit seemed to be in a hurry. He took a watch from his pocket and Alice heard him say that he would be late. She wondered what the white rabbit would be late for, so she decided to follow him.

愛麗絲夢遊仙境

愛麗絲發現一隻白兔子並且發現一個新世界

愛麗絲和她的姊姊坐在河邊。愛麗絲很無聊。她的姊姊正在讀一本書,而愛麗絲卻沒事做。她又熱又累,就要開始睡覺時,她聽見一個聲響。她往上看,看到了一隻白色的兔子。那隻兔子好像很匆忙。他從口袋裡拿出一個手錶,同時愛麗絲聽見他說,他要遲到了。她想知道那隻白兔子什麼事會遲到,所以她決定要跟蹤他。

Alice ran after the rabbit who disappeared down a rabbit- hole. Without thinking, Alice followed. Inside the hole, she found herself falling and falling and falling.

Alice started to think about where she was going. Maybe she would land in the center of the earth, maybe in Australia. Suddenly she did land on a pile of leaves. Fortunately she was not hurt. She saw the rabbit running down a passage and she quickly followed him.

However, as she went around the corner she found that the rabbit had disappeared.

愛麗絲在兔子後面跑，兔子從下面的一個兔子洞消失不見了。想也不想，愛麗絲跟在後頭。在洞裡，她發現自己往下掉、往下掉、往下掉。愛麗絲開始想著她會到哪裡去。也許她會著陸在地心，也許在澳洲。突然間她真的著陸了，掉在一堆葉子上。很幸運，她並沒有受傷。她看見那隻兔子跑下一條通道，她就很快地跟著他。

不過，當她跑到角落附近時，她發現那隻兔子已經不見了。

Now she was lost! Alice looked around. There was a table and many doors, but they were all locked. Finally Alice found a key on the table.

The key opened the smallest door that led to a garden. The door was too small and Alice was too big to get through. Then, she saw a bottle on the floor. It said "drink me", so she did. Alice felt very strange. She realized that she was getting smaller. Now she was only 10 inches high.

現在她迷路了！愛麗絲看看四周。有一張桌子和許多門，但是門都上了鎖。最後，愛麗絲在桌子上找到了一把鑰匙。

那把鑰匙打開了最小的一扇門，這扇門通向一個花園。這扇門太小了，而愛麗絲太大了，所以走不過去。然後，她看見地板上有一個瓶子。瓶子上寫著「喝我吧」，於是她就照做了。愛麗絲感到非常奇怪。她明白原來她愈變愈小了。現在她只有十英吋高。

Alice was small enough to get through the door and into the garden. Suddenly she remembered that she had left the key on the table, but now she was too small to reach it. Alice started to cry. She sat down on the floor and by her feet she saw a small cake. It said "eat me" on the cake, so she did.

愛麗絲小到足以穿過那扇門進到花園去了。突然間，她想起她把那把鑰匙留在桌子上了，可是她現在太矮，搆不到桌子了。愛麗絲哭了起來。她坐在地板上，而就在她的腳邊，她看見一個小蛋糕。蛋糕上寫著「吃我吧」，所以她就照做了。

ALICE EATS SOME CAKE AND CHANGES SIZE

After she had eaten the cake, Alice started to grow. Soon, she was so tall her head hit the roof of the passage. She took the key from the table and opened the door. However, now she was too big to get through! Alice started to cry again. Big tears fell from her face and made a very large pool of water on the floor.

愛麗絲吃了一些蛋糕並且改變大小

在她吃過蛋糕之後，愛麗絲開始長大起來。很快地，她長得很高，她的頭都撞到那條通道的屋頂了。她從桌子上拿了那把鑰匙，然後打開門。可是呢，她太高了，所以走不過去！愛麗絲又哭了起來。大顆的淚珠從她的臉上掉下來，結果在地板上弄成一個非常大的水池。

Just then, the white rabbit appeared. He was still in a hurry and Alice heard him say that the Duchess would be angry if he was late. Alice was so unhappy. She asked the rabbit for help. The rabbit was surprised and scared because Alice was so big. He ran away as fast as he could leaving his gloves and his fan behind. Alice picked up the fan. Immediately she began to get smaller and smaller. Soon she was only 2 foot high. However, now she found herself up to her chin in water. The water was her own tears!

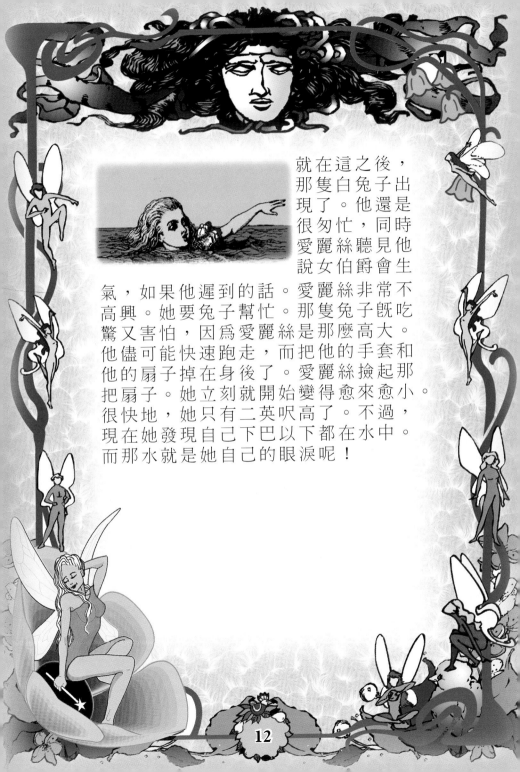

就在這之後，那隻白兔子出現了。他還是很匆忙，同時愛麗絲聽見他說女伯爵會生氣，如果他遲到的話。愛麗絲非常不高興。她要兔子幫忙。那隻兔子既驚又害怕，因為愛麗絲是那麼高大。他儘可能快速跑走，而把他的手套和他的扇子掉在身後了。愛麗絲撿起那把扇子。她立刻就開始變得愈來愈小。很快地，她只有二英呎高了。不過，現在她發現自己下巴以下都在水中。而那水就是她自己的眼淚呢！

As she swam around she saw that she was not alone. She looked closer. It was a mouse. Then she saw a duck, a dodo an eaglet and many other creatures. Alice decided that they should all get out of the water and she lead them to the water's edge.

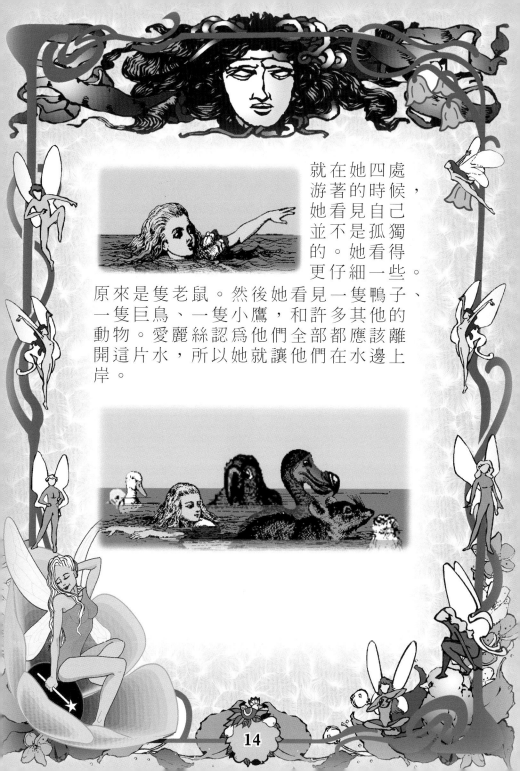

就在她四處游著的時候，她看見自己並不是孤獨的。她看得更仔細一些。原來是隻老鼠。然後她看見一隻鴨子、一隻巨鳥、一隻小鷹，和許多其他的動物。愛麗絲認為他們全部都應該離開這片水，所以她就讓他們在水邊上岸。

ALICE AND THE ANIMALS PLAY GAMES

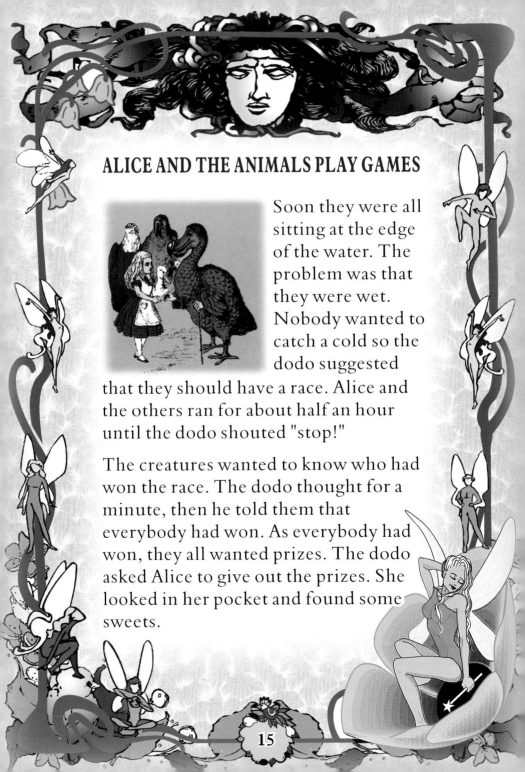

Soon they were all sitting at the edge of the water. The problem was that they were wet. Nobody wanted to catch a cold so the dodo suggested that they should have a race. Alice and the others ran for about half an hour until the dodo shouted "stop!"

The creatures wanted to know who had won the race. The dodo thought for a minute, then he told them that everybody had won. As everybody had won, they all wanted prizes. The dodo asked Alice to give out the prizes. She looked in her pocket and found some sweets.

愛麗絲和動物們比賽

很快地，他們全部都坐在水邊上了。問題是，他們都弄濕了。因為沒有人想要感冒，所以巨鳥就建議說他們應該來個賽跑。愛麗絲和其他動物跑了大約半小時，直到巨鳥喊「停」為止。

那些動物們想知道誰贏了賽跑。巨鳥想了一分鐘，然後他告訴他們每個人都贏了。因為每個人都贏了，所以他們全部都要獎品。巨鳥就叫愛麗絲頒發獎品。她看著她的口袋，發現了一些糖果。

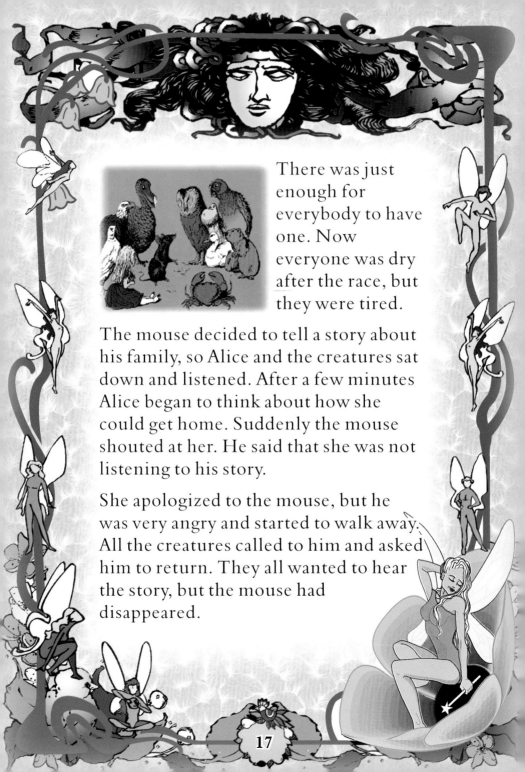

There was just enough for everybody to have one. Now everyone was dry after the race, but they were tired.

The mouse decided to tell a story about his family, so Alice and the creatures sat down and listened. After a few minutes Alice began to think about how she could get home. Suddenly the mouse shouted at her. He said that she was not listening to his story.

She apologized to the mouse, but he was very angry and started to walk away. All the creatures called to him and asked him to return. They all wanted to hear the story, but the mouse had disappeared.

正好夠給每一個
人一個。現在在
賽跑後，每個人
都乾了，不過他
們也累了。

老鼠想要說一個
關於他家的故事，
於是愛麗絲和其他動物就坐下來聽。
過了幾分鐘之後，愛麗絲開始想著她
怎麼樣才能回家。突然間，老鼠對著
她大叫。他說她沒有在聽他的故事。

雖然她向老鼠道歉，但是他還是非常
生氣，便開始離去。所有的動物都叫
他，要他回來。他們都想聽他的故事
，但是老鼠卻不見了。

The mouse's story reminded Alice of her cat, Dinah, who was waiting for her at home. She told the others about her cat and how she wished her cat was with them.

Now, this caused a problem as Alice's cat liked to eat birds. The other creatures, especially the birds were very unhappy with what Alice had said. One by one they made excuses and left. Soon Alice was all alone.

老鼠的故事讓愛麗絲想起她的貓－－迪那，牠正在家裡等著她。她便告訴其他動物關於她的貓的事，還有她多麼希望她的貓也跟他們在一起。

現在，這又造成了一個問題，因為愛麗絲的貓喜歡吃鳥類。其他的動物，特別是鳥類非常不高興聽到愛麗絲所說的。他們一個接著一個藉口離去了。很快地，愛麗絲完全孤獨了。

ALICE FINDS THE WHITE RABBIT'S HOUSE

Alice heard footsteps. She hoped that it was the mouse and the other creatures coming back to finish the story. It wasn't, it was the white rabbit. He was still in a hurry and talking to himself about how the Duchess would execute him if he kept her waiting.

When he saw Alice, he shouted to her "Mary Ann, get my gloves and my fan!"

The rabbit pointed into the distance. Alice was so scared she ran off in the direction that he was pointing.

愛麗絲發現白兔子的家

愛麗絲聽到有腳步聲。她希望那是老鼠和其他動物回來說完故事。那不是,那是那隻白兔子。他還是很匆忙,而且自言自語著女伯爵會如何處置他,萬一他讓她一直等待。

當他看見愛麗絲時,他對她大叫道:「瑪莉'安,去拿我的手套和我的扇子!」

那隻兔子指著遠方。愛麗絲好害怕,所以她就朝著他所指的方向跑過去。

She went inside and found the bedroom. She picked up a pair of gloves and a fan. Just as she was about to leave she saw another bottle. It also had "drink me" written on it. Alice thought it might make her big again so she drank it. Sure enough, she started to grow. Unfortunately though, Alice grew too big. She could not get out of the rabbit's house!

Alice laid down on the floor and she tried to think of what to do. Then, she heard the rabbit's voice. He was asking for his gloves and his fan. The white rabbit tried to open the front door. He couldn't open it because Alice was too big. He decided to try and get into the house through the window.

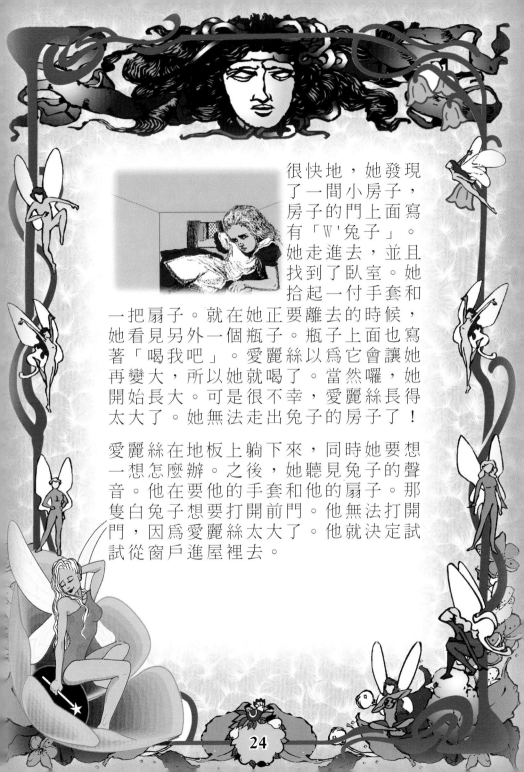

很快地，她發現了一間小房子，房子的門上面寫有「W'兔子」。她走進去，並且找到了臥室。她拾起一付手套和一把扇子。就在她正要離去的時候，她看見另外一個瓶子。瓶子上面也寫著「喝我吧」。愛麗絲以為它會讓她再變大，所以她就喝了。當然囉，她開始長大。可是很不幸，愛麗絲長得太大了。她無法走出兔子的房子了！

愛麗絲在地板上躺下來，同時她要想一想怎麼辦。之後，她聽見兔子的聲音。他在要他的手套和他的扇子。那隻白兔子想要打開前門。他無法打開門，因為愛麗絲太大了。他就決定試試從窗戶進屋裡去。

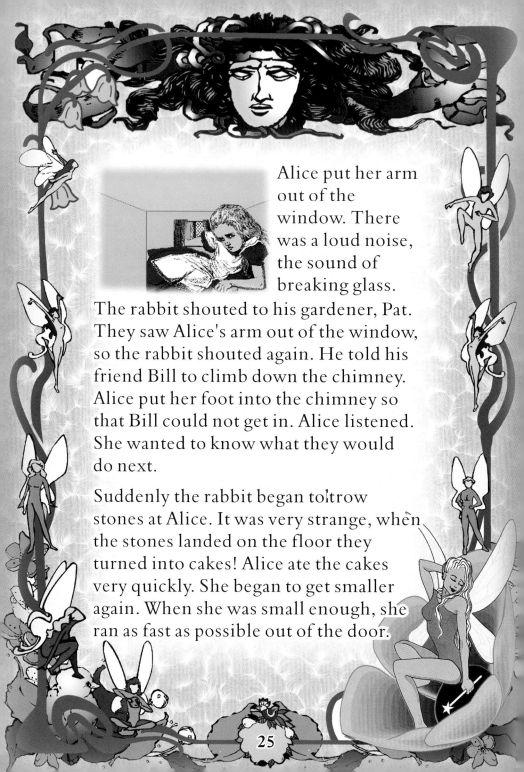

Alice put her arm out of the window. There was a loud noise, the sound of breaking glass. The rabbit shouted to his gardener, Pat. They saw Alice's arm out of the window, so the rabbit shouted again. He told his friend Bill to climb down the chimney. Alice put her foot into the chimney so that Bill could not get in. Alice listened. She wanted to know what they would do next.

Suddenly the rabbit began to throw stones at Alice. It was very strange, when the stones landed on the floor they turned into cakes! Alice ate the cakes very quickly. She began to get smaller again. When she was small enough, she ran as fast as possible out of the door.

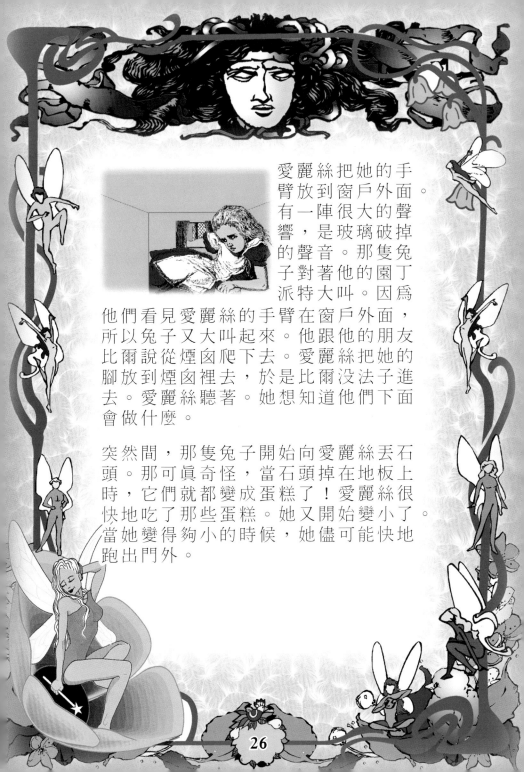

愛麗絲把她的手臂放到窗戶外面。有一陣很大的聲響，是玻璃破掉的聲音。那隻兔子對著他的園丁派特大叫。因為他們看見愛麗絲的手臂在窗戶外面，所以兔子又大叫起來。他跟他的朋友比爾說從煙囪爬下去。愛麗絲把她的腳放到煙囪裡去，於是比爾沒法子進去。愛麗絲聽著。她想知道他們下面會做什麼。

突然間，那隻兔子開始向愛麗絲丟石頭。那可真奇怪，當石頭掉在地板上時，它們就都變成蛋糕了！愛麗絲很快地吃了那些蛋糕。她又開始變小了。當她變得夠小的時候，她儘可能快地跑出門外。

The rabbit and the others ran towards Alice, but she ran very quickly into the woods. Once in the woods Alice tried to think of a way to return to her normal size. As she was walking she found a large mushroom growing in the wood. Sitting on the top was a caterpillar.

那隻兔子和其他人朝愛麗絲跑去，但是她很快就跑進林子裡去了。一到林子裡，愛麗絲就試著想辦法變回她正常的大小。當她正在走著的時候，她發現林子裡長著一個大蘑菇。坐在上面的是一隻毛毛蟲。

THE CATERPILLAR

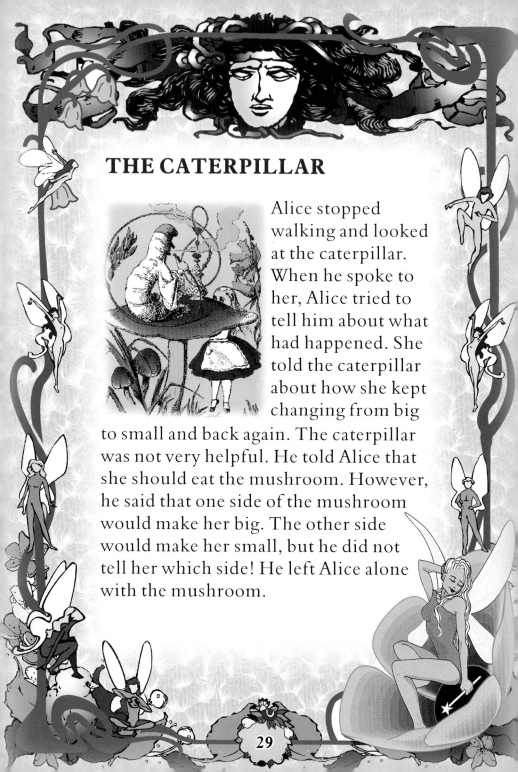

Alice stopped walking and looked at the caterpillar. When he spoke to her, Alice tried to tell him about what had happened. She told the caterpillar about how she kept changing from big to small and back again. The caterpillar was not very helpful. He told Alice that she should eat the mushroom. However, he said that one side of the mushroom would make her big. The other side would make her small, but he did not tell her which side! He left Alice alone with the mushroom.

毛毛蟲

走毛說不她對那隻毛毛蟲從來不是很高興。那隻不斷回變不是很告訴那她發生的那隻毛毛蟲如何變小，又不是毛毛蟲告訴她應該吃那一半會讓她應上忙。他告訴她應該吃那一半會讓愛麗絲幫得上忙。他告訴她應該吃那愛麗絲停下來看著那隻毛毛蟲。當他對她說話的時候，愛麗絲就想告訴他那隻不斷回變不是很告訴那她如何變小，又變不了。她告訴那隻毛毛蟲她大變小，那隻毛毛蟲幫得上忙。他告訴愛麗絲

個蘑菇。不過，他說蘑菇的一半會讓
她變大。另外一半會讓她變小，但是
他沒有告訴她是哪一半！他讓愛麗絲
獨自與那蘑菇在一起。

Alice stood there and looked at the mushroom. She tried to decide which part to eat. She took a piece from the left side and a piece from the right side. She started to eat one piece. Suddenly she felt herself getting smaller. Soon her chin was touching her feet. Very quickly she ate the other piece. Alice started to grow again. However, she soon realized that only her neck was growing.

At that moment a pigeon flew past and screamed "serpent!"

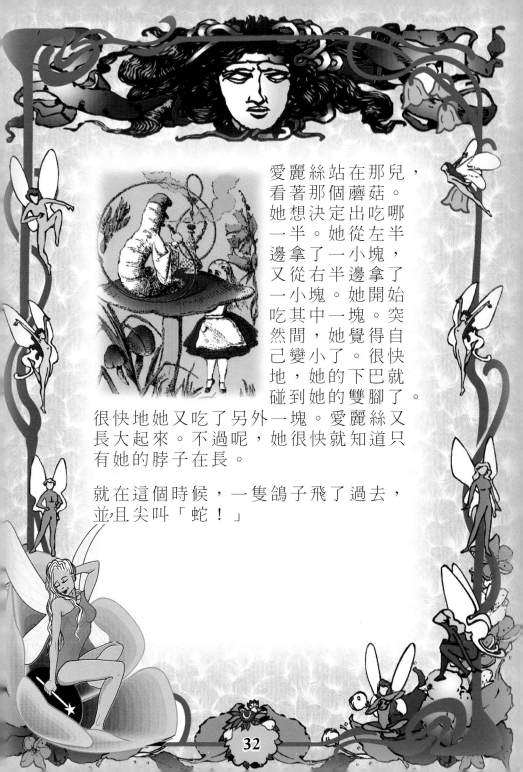

愛麗絲站在那兒，看著那個蘑菇。她想決定出吃哪一半。她從左半邊拿了一小塊，又從右半邊拿了一小塊。她開始吃其中一塊。突然間，她覺得自己變小了。很快地，她的下巴就碰到她的雙腳了。

很快地她又吃了另外一塊。愛麗絲又長大起來。不過呢，她很快就知道只有她的脖子在長。

就在這個時候，一隻鴿子飛了過去，並且尖叫「蛇！」

Alice was angry. She explained to the pigeon that she was a little girl, not a serpent. The pigeon did not believe her. He was worried that Alice wanted to eat his eggs. He complained that serpents always ate his eggs. Alice promised that she would not eat the pigeon's eggs. She told him that she did not eat raw eggs. The pigeon was still not happy, but he flew back to his nest.

愛麗絲非常生氣。她向那隻鴿子解釋說她是一個小女孩，不是一條小蛇。那隻鴿子不相信她。他很擔心愛麗絲想吃他的蛋。他解釋說愛麗絲答應不會吃鴿子的蛋。她告訴他她不吃的蛋。雖然那隻鴿子還是不高興，但是他飛回他的鳥窩去了。

Alice remembered that she still had some pieces of mushroom. First she ate bit from the left side, then from the right. Slowly she began to return to her normal size. Alice continued to walk through the woods until she saw a very small house. She decided to eat more of the mushroom to make her small again. She did not want to scare the people in the house by being very large.

愛麗絲想起來她還有一些蘑菇塊。起先，她吃了左半邊的一小塊，然後吃右半邊。慢慢地，她開始回到她正常的大小了。愛麗絲繼續步行穿過林子，一直到她看見一幢很小的房子為止。她決定多吃一些蘑菇，以便讓她再變小。她不想嚇到房子裡的人，因為她很大。

ALICE MEETS THE DUCHESS AND THE CHESHIRE CAT

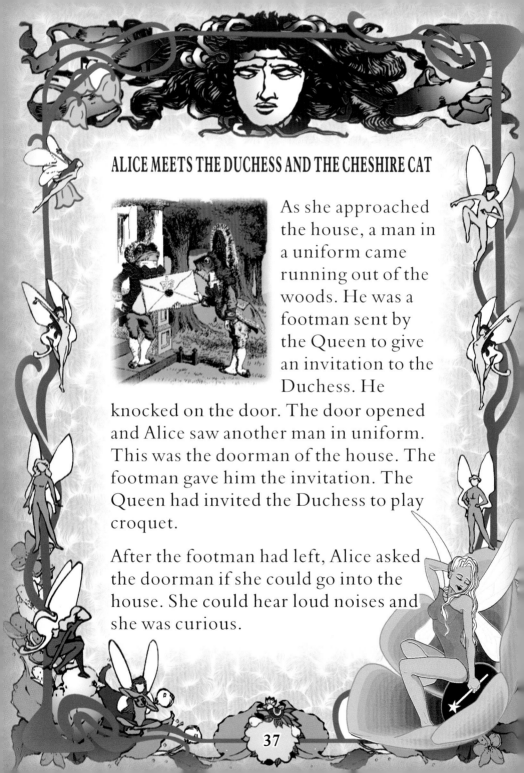

As she approached the house, a man in a uniform came running out of the woods. He was a footman sent by the Queen to give an invitation to the Duchess. He knocked on the door. The door opened and Alice saw another man in uniform. This was the doorman of the house. The footman gave him the invitation. The Queen had invited the Duchess to play croquet.

After the footman had left, Alice asked the doorman if she could go into the house. She could hear loud noises and she was curious.

愛麗絲遇見女伯爵和赤郡貓

當她朝房子前進時，一個穿著制服的人從林子裡跑出來。他是皇后派來的一個男僕人，要去給女伯爵送邀請函。他敲敲門。門開了，愛麗絲看見另一個穿著制服的人。這是那個房子的門房。那個男僕人把邀請函給他。皇后邀請女伯爵去打槌球。

在那個男僕人離去後，愛麗絲就問那個門房，她是否可以進房子裡去。她聽見有很大的聲響，她很好奇。

The doorman was not very helpful, so Alice knocked on the door. Just then, the door opened and a large plate came flying out. It almost hit the doorman on the head. He did nothing.

Alice thought he was crazy. She opened the door again and went inside. There was a large kitchen. The Duchess and a baby were sitting at the kitchen table. There was a cook making soup and a Cheshire cat on the floor.

那個門房幫不上忙，所以愛麗絲就敲門了。就在這個時候，門開了，一個大盤子飛了出來。它幾乎打到那個門房的頭。他什麼也不做。

愛麗絲認為他發瘋了。她又打開門，然後走到裡面去。有一個大廚房呢。女伯爵和一個娃娃坐在廚房桌旁。有一個廚師正在煮湯，還有一隻赤郡貓在地板上。

He had the biggest smile Alice had ever seen. Suddenly the cook took the saucepans and the plates and started throwing them. The baby screamed, but the Duchess took no notice. Alice was scared. She jumped in the air and told the cook to stop throwing the saucepans and plates.

The Duchess was angry with Alice for shouting at the cook. She told her she would chop off her head.

愛麗絲露出她最燦爛的笑容。突然那個廚師拿起平底鍋和盤子，然後開始丟。那個娃娃尖叫起來，不過女伯爵卻

不去注意。愛麗絲很害怕。她跳呀跳的，並且告訴那個廚師不要再丟鍋子和盤子。

女伯爵很氣愛麗絲，因為她對著廚師大叫。她告訴她要把她的頭砍掉。

Then the Duchess started to sing and she threw the baby in the air. Soon she was bored. She gave the baby to Alice and said she was going to play croquet with the Queen. The baby began to make very strange noises. Alice looked at it closely. It's face was quite unusual. In fact, it looked just like a pig! Quickly Alice put the baby on the floor and left the house.

Outside she saw the Cheshire cat, still smiling and sitting in a tree.

之後，女伯爵開始唱歌，並且把娃娃向上丟。很快地，她覺得不好玩了。她把娃娃交給愛麗絲，並且說她要去和皇后打槌球。那個娃娃開始發出很奇怪的噪音。愛麗絲仔細地看著他。他的臉好不尋常呀。

事實上，它看起來就像隻豬！很快地，愛麗絲把那個娃娃放在地上，然後離開了那幢房子。

在外面，她看見了那隻赤郡貓，還在笑著，同時坐在一棵樹上。

44

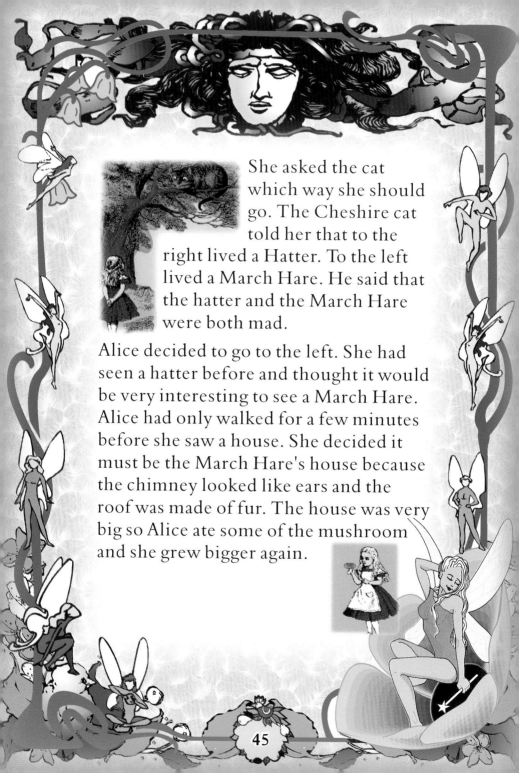

She asked the cat which way she should go. The Cheshire cat told her that to the right lived a Hatter. To the left lived a March Hare. He said that the hatter and the March Hare were both mad.

Alice decided to go to the left. She had seen a hatter before and thought it would be very interesting to see a March Hare. Alice had only walked for a few minutes before she saw a house. She decided it must be the March Hare's house because the chimney looked like ears and the roof was made of fur. The house was very big so Alice ate some of the mushroom and she grew bigger again.

她便問那隻貓，她應該走哪一條路。那隻赤郡貓跟她說，右邊住著一個賣帽子的人。而左邊住著一隻三月兔。他說那個賣帽子的人和那隻三月兔兩個都瘋了。

愛麗絲想要走左邊。她從前看過一個賣帽子的人了，所以她想去看一隻三月兔會很有趣。愛麗絲才走了幾分鐘，她就看見一幢房子了。她想那一定是三月兔的房子，因為煙囪看起來像耳朵，而屋頂是毛皮做的。那幢房子很大，所以愛麗絲便吃了一些蘑菇，然後她又變大了。

THE MAD HATTER'S TEA PARTY

Outside the house was a table. The March Hare and the Hatter sat at the table drinking tea. A Dormouse was asleep next to them. The table was very big, but all three were sitting close together at one end.

Alice sat down at the other end. The March Hare told her that she was impolite because she had not been invited.

瘋狂賣帽子人的茶會

房子外面有一張桌子。三月兔和賣帽子的人坐在桌旁喝茶。一隻榛睡鼠在他們旁邊睡覺。那張桌子很大，不過那三個全都緊緊坐在一頭。

愛麗絲在另一頭坐下。三月兔跟她說她不太禮貌，因為她並沒有受到邀請。

The Hatter told Alice that her hair was not pretty. Alice thought they were very rude. Alice noticed that the March Hare had a very unusual watch. It did not tell the time! She asked why. The Hatter told her the story. He said that last March the Queen of Hearts had given a concert. The Queen had asked the March Hare to sing.

While he was singing, the Queen had shouted "off with his head!".

賣帽子的人跟愛麗絲說她的頭髮不好看。愛麗絲認爲他們很粗魯。愛麗絲注意到三月兔有一支很不尋常的手錶。它不指出時間呢！她問爲什麼。賣帽子的人跟她說這個故事。他說去年三月紅桃皇后給了一場音樂會。皇后要三月兔去唱歌。

而就在他唱歌的時候，皇后卻大吼「把他的頭砍了！」

After this the March Hare had gone mad, he would never look at the time. He said it was always 6 o'clock - tea time. Now the March Hare wanted Alice to tell a story. Alice thought that the Dormouse could tell good stories. The Hatter and the March Hare agreed. They woke the Dormouse and asked him to tell a story.

在這件事之後，三月兔就發瘋了，他
絕對不看時間了。他說時間永遠都是
六點鐘 —— 吃飯時間。現在三月兔
要愛麗絲說一個故事。麗絲卻認為那
隻榛睡鼠會有很好的故事。賣帽子人
和三月兔都同意。他們叫醒榛睡鼠，
並且要他說個故事。

However, the Dormouse was very tired. He started to tell his story, but it was nonsense. Alice asked many questions, but the March Hare and the Hatter were very rude to her. This made her angry so she stood up and walked away.

Alice agreed with the Cheshire cat the March Hare and the Hatter were both mad. Alice walked through the woods until she saw a door.

不過呢，那隻榛睡鼠好累呀。他開始
說他的故事，但是都是胡說八道。愛
麗絲問了許多問題，可是三月兔和賣
帽子的人對他卻很兇。這讓她好生氣，
所以她站起來走掉了。

愛麗絲步行穿過林子，一直到她看見
一扇門為止。

She thought
it was very
odd that
there was a
door in the
middle of
the woods,
but she went in anyway. She found that
she was back in the passage with the
table and many doors. She took the key
from the table and ate some of the
mushroom. She became smaller and
smaller. Finally she could get through
the door. Finally she could enter the
beautiful garden.

林中央有很多事，她還是回子上有一個怪的門，她進去。她發現桌子上蘑菇。認為正是她的進去。她發現有著桌子。她子一個奇怪但是走了。她發現有從桌子上一些蘑菇。可以穿過那個美麗

和許多門的那條通道了。她從桌子上一些蘑菇。可以穿過拿了那把鑰匙，並且吃了一些蘑菇。她變得愈來愈小。最後，她可以進到那個美麗那扇門。最後，她可以進到那個美麗的花園去了。

56

THE QUEEN'S GARDEN

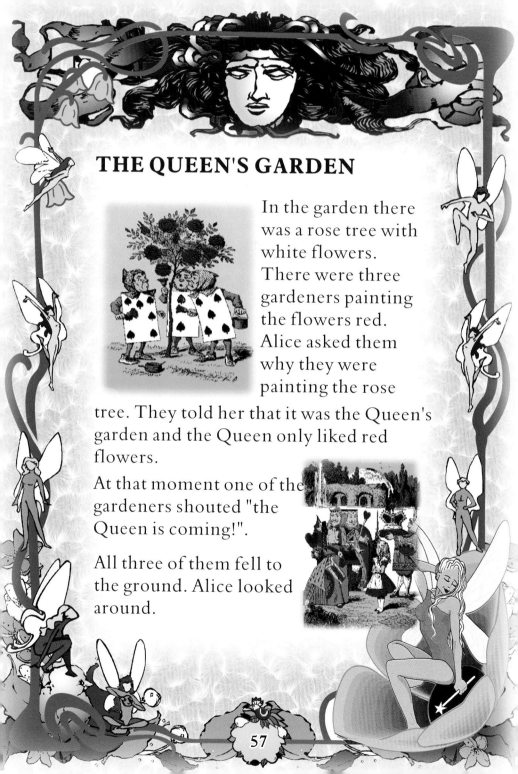

In the garden there was a rose tree with white flowers. There were three gardeners painting the flowers red. Alice asked them why they were painting the rose tree. They told her that it was the Queen's garden and the Queen only liked red flowers.

At that moment one of the gardeners shouted "the Queen is coming!".

All three of them fell to the ground. Alice looked around.

皇后的花園

在那個花園裡，有一株玫瑰開著白色的花。有三個園丁在把花漆成紅色。愛麗絲問他們為什麼把那株玫瑰漆成紅色。他們跟她說那是皇后的花園，而皇后只喜歡紅色的花。

就在這個時候，其中一個園丁大叫「皇后駕到！」。

他們三個人全都倒到地上。愛麗絲看看四周。

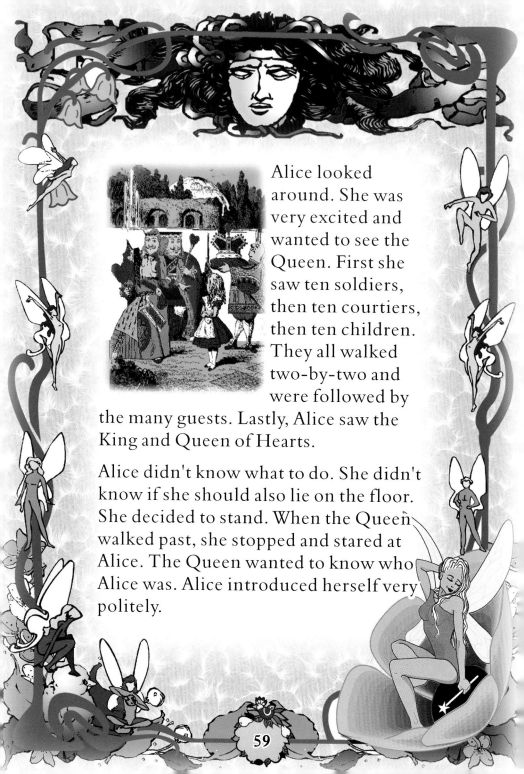

Alice looked around. She was very excited and wanted to see the Queen. First she saw ten soldiers, then ten courtiers, then ten children. They all walked two-by-two and were followed by the many guests. Lastly, Alice saw the King and Queen of Hearts.

Alice didn't know what to do. She didn't know if she should also lie on the floor. She decided to stand. When the Queen walked past, she stopped and stared at Alice. The Queen wanted to know who Alice was. Alice introduced herself very politely.

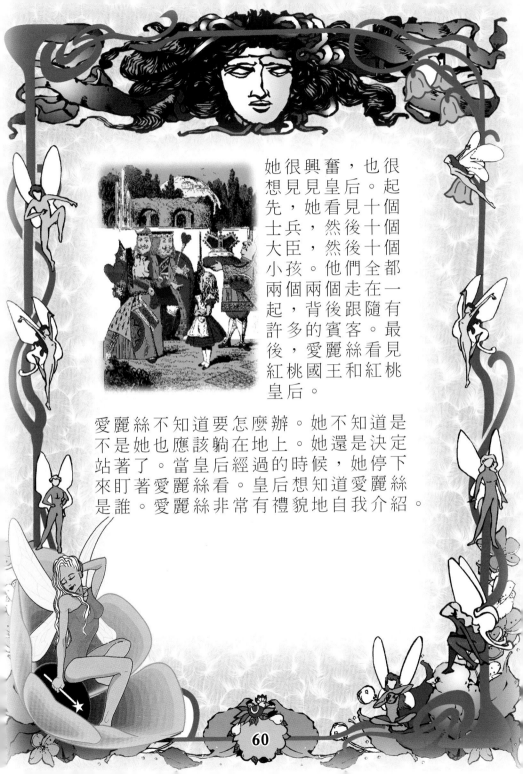

她很興奮，也很想見見皇后。起先，她看見十個士兵，然後十個大臣，然後十個小孩。他們全都兩個兩個走在一起，背後跟隨有許多的賓客。最後，愛麗絲看見紅桃國王和紅桃皇后。

愛麗絲不知道要怎麼辦。她不知道是不是她也應該躺在地上。她還是決定站著了。當皇后經過的時候，她停下來盯著愛麗絲看。皇后想知道愛麗絲是誰。愛麗絲非常有禮貌地自我介紹。

Then the Queen wanted to know who the three people lying on the floor were.

Alice said she didn't know, which made the Queen very angry and she shouted "off with her head!"

Now Alice was angry and she shouted "Nonsense!"

The Queen looked at the gardeners who were still lying on the ground.

"Off with their heads!" she shouted and walked away leaving three soldiers to execute them.

然後皇后想要知道躺在地上的那三個人是誰。

愛麗絲說她不知道，這讓皇后非常生氣，所以她說「把她的頭砍了！」

現在，愛麗絲生氣了，她大叫「胡說八道！」

皇后看著那些園丁，他們還躺在地上。

「把他們的頭砍了！」她大吼並且走開，留下三個士兵來處置他們。

Quickly Alice hid the gardeners. When the soldiers could not find them they left.

The Queen shouted to Alice again. This time she asked Alice if she could play croquet. Alice told her she could and joined the Queen as she walked. The white rabbit was also there. Very quietly he told Alice that the Queen and the Duchess had argued that morning. The Queen was still very angry about this and she ordered everyone to play croquet.

很快地，愛麗絲就把園丁們藏起來了。就在士兵們找不到他們的時候，他們就離開了。

皇后又對著愛麗絲大吼。這一次她問愛麗絲是不是會打槌球。愛麗絲跟她說她會，同時跟著皇后一起走了。那隻白兔子也在那裡。悄悄地，他告訴愛麗絲皇后和女伯爵那天早上吵架了。皇后還在生氣這件事，所以她命令每個人都打槌球。

Alice was very surprised at the croquet pitch. The mallets were flamingoes and the balls were hedgehogs. This made it very difficult to play and Alice couldn't help laughing.

The Queen marched around the croquet pitch shouting "Off with their heads" to the players.

Alice began to get worried. Maybe she would be the next to lose her head. She decided to try and escape. Just then, the head of the Cheshire cat appeared.

愛麗絲在槌球場吃了一驚。木槌是紅鶴，而球是刺蝟。這讓打球變得很困難，而且愛麗絲不能不笑。

皇后在槌球場四處行走，對著打球的人大叫著「把他們的頭砍了！」

愛麗絲擔心起來。也許她會是下一個掉了頭的人。她想試試看逃走。就在這個時候，赤郡貓的頭出現了。

Alice was glad. Now she had someone nice to talk to. The Cheshire cat asked Alice if she liked the Queen. Alice was about to say the answer when the King arrived.

He did not like the Cheshire cat and so he called to the Queen who said "Off with its head".

The King went to find the executioner.

Alice returned to the game, but the hedgehogs were fighting and the flamingoes were trying to fly into the trees.

愛麗絲很高興。現在，她有個不錯的人可以說說話了。赤郡貓問愛麗絲是否喜歡皇后。愛麗絲就要說出回答時，國王到了。

他不喜歡赤郡貓，所以他就呼喚皇后，而皇后便說

「把牠的頭砍了！」

國王便去找劊子手。

愛麗絲回到球賽去，但是刺蝟們正在打架，而紅鶴們正想飛到樹林裡去。

Alice gave up. By this time the King and the executioner had come back. Many people were standing around the Cheshire cat. They were arguing. The executioner argued that you could not cut off a head unless there was a body. The King argued that if there was a head, there must be a body. The Queen argued that everybody should be executed.

They asked Alice what to do. Alice said that because the Cheshire cat belonged to the Duchess, they should ask the Duchess what to do.

愛麗絲放棄了。就在這個時候，國王和劊子手回來了。許多人站著圍住赤郡貓。他們在吵架。劊子手吵著說不可以砍頭，除非有一個身體。國王吵著說如果有頭，一定有一個身體。皇后吵著說每個人都應該處斬。

他們問愛麗絲要怎麼辦。愛麗絲說因為赤郡貓屬於女伯爵所有，他們可以去問女伯爵該怎麼辦。

However, the Duchess was in prison. The Queen had sent her there after their argument. She told the executioner to run to the prison and get the Duchess.

不過呢，女伯爵
被關在監獄裡。
皇后在他們吵架
之後把她送進監
獄了。她告訴劊
子手跑到監獄去
帶女伯爵來。

ALICE PLAYS CROQUET AND MEETS THE MOCK TURTLE

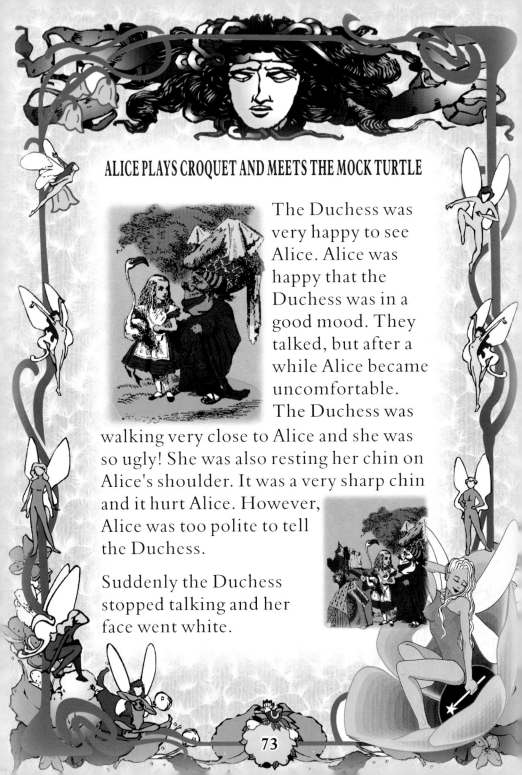

The Duchess was very happy to see Alice. Alice was happy that the Duchess was in a good mood. They talked, but after a while Alice became uncomfortable. The Duchess was walking very close to Alice and she was so ugly! She was also resting her chin on Alice's shoulder. It was a very sharp chin and it hurt Alice. However, Alice was too polite to tell the Duchess.

Suddenly the Duchess stopped talking and her face went white.

愛麗絲打槌球並且碰到假烏龜

女伯爵很高興看見愛麗絲。愛麗絲很高興，因為女伯爵心情很好。他們交談，但是過了一會兒後，愛麗絲又不太舒服了。女伯爵走得非常靠近愛麗絲，而她是那麼的醜啊！她還把她的下巴靠在愛麗絲的肩膀上。那是一個很尖的下巴，它把愛麗絲弄痛了。雖然如此，愛麗絲還是很有禮貌，不敢跟女伯爵說。

突然間，女伯爵停止說話，她的臉也變白了。

74

The Queen had arrived. The Queen stamped her foot and told the Duchess to leave. If she didn't leave, the Queen would chop her head off. Before Alice could do anything, the Duchess had disappeared.

The Queen then ordered Alice to play croquet and because she was scared, Alice agreed. The game did not last very long, though. The Queen wanted to execute all the players. Soon there was only the King, Queen and Alice left.

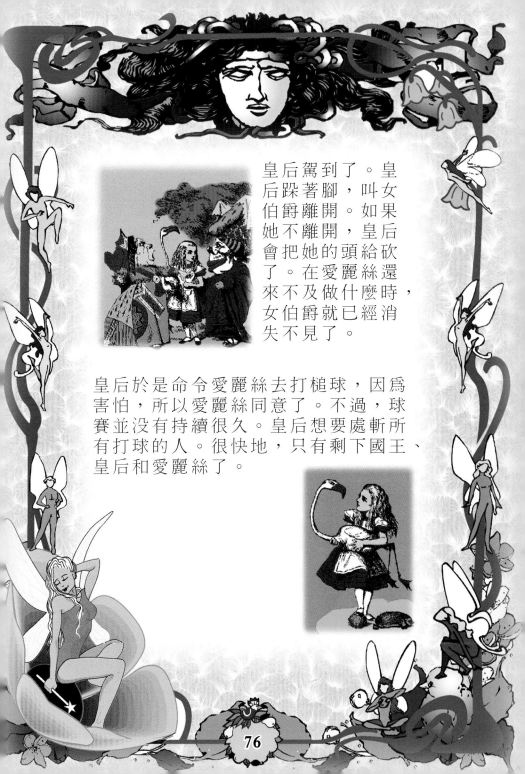

皇后駕到了。皇后跺著腳，叫女伯爵離開。如果她不離開，皇后會把她的頭給砍了。在愛麗絲還來不及做什麼時，女伯爵就已經消失不見了。

皇后於是命令愛麗絲去打槌球，因爲害怕，所以愛麗絲同意了。不過，球賽並沒有持續很久。皇后想要處斬所有打球的人。很快地，只有剩下國王、皇后和愛麗絲了。

However, as Alice and the Queen walked away, Alice heard the King tell the players that they could go home.

Alice was very happy that they were not going to be executed. The Queen asked Alice if she had met the Mock Turtle. Alice had not, so the Queen asked one of her servants to take Alice to the Mock Turtle. When Alice arrived, he was sitting on a rock. He looked very sad.

雖然如此，當愛麗絲和皇后走開的時候，愛麗絲聽見國王告訴打球的人說他們可以回家。

愛麗絲很高興，因為他們不會被處斬。皇后問愛麗絲有沒有碰到假烏龜。愛麗絲沒碰到他，於是皇后就叫她的一個僕人帶愛麗絲去找假烏龜。當愛麗絲到達的時候，他正坐在一個石頭上。他看起來很傷心。那個僕人告訴愛麗絲說假烏龜看起來總是很傷心。

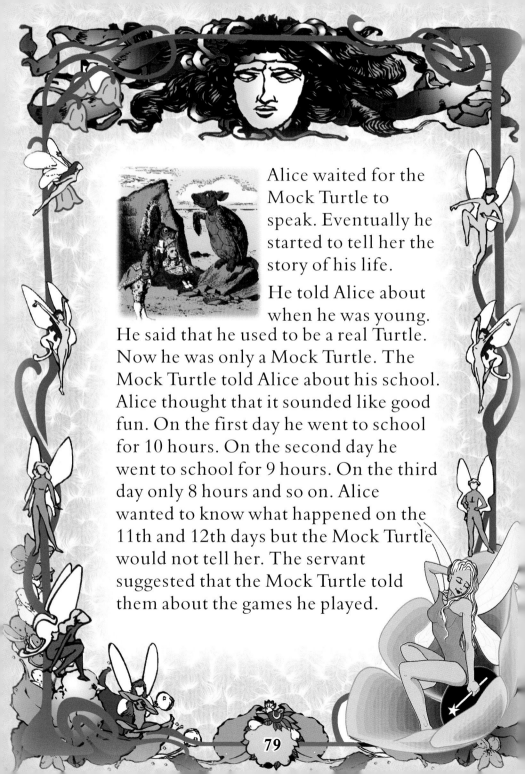

Alice waited for the Mock Turtle to speak. Eventually he started to tell her the story of his life.

He told Alice about when he was young. He said that he used to be a real Turtle. Now he was only a Mock Turtle. The Mock Turtle told Alice about his school. Alice thought that it sounded like good fun. On the first day he went to school for 10 hours. On the second day he went to school for 9 hours. On the third day only 8 hours and so on. Alice wanted to know what happened on the 11th and 12th days but the Mock Turtle would not tell her. The servant suggested that the Mock Turtle told them about the games he played.

愛麗絲等假烏龜開口說話。最後他終於把他一生的故事告訴她。

他跟愛麗絲說他年輕時候的事。他說他本來是一隻真的烏龜。而現在他只是一隻假烏龜了。假烏龜跟愛麗絲說他學校的事。愛麗絲認為那聽起來很好玩。第一天他去學校去了十小時。第二天他去學校去了九小時。第三天只去了八小時等等。愛麗絲想知道第十一天和第十二天怎麼了，但是假烏龜不肯告訴她。那個僕人建議他跟他們說他玩過的遊戲。

THE TRIAL

The Mock Turtle began to cry. He was always sad when he talked about his life. He started to talk about the Lobster Quadrille. This was a dance. All the fish would dance by the sea. They would throw the lobsters into the sea and swim after them. Then they would swim back to the shore.

The Mock Turtle and the servant wanted to show Alice the dance. There were no lobsters so it was quite difficult. The Mock Turtle began to sing and they both danced.

審　問

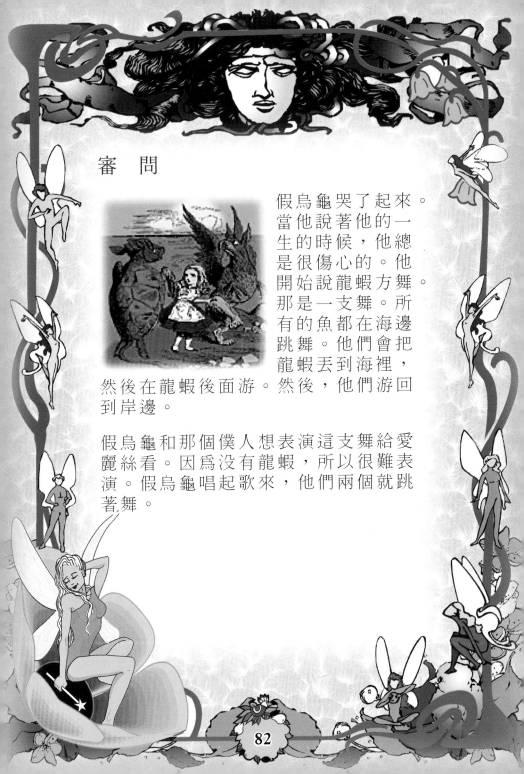

假烏龜哭了起來。
當他說著他的一
生的時候，他總
是很傷心的。他
開始說龍蝦方舞。
那是一支舞。所
有的魚都在海邊
跳舞。他們會把
龍蝦丟到海裡，
然後在龍蝦後面游。然後，他們游回
到岸邊。

假烏龜和那個僕人想表演這支舞給愛
麗絲看。因為沒有龍蝦，所以很難表
演。假烏龜唱起歌來，他們兩個就跳
著舞。

While they danced the servant and the Mock Turtle trod on Alice's toes. Alice was happy when they finished dancing because her feet were now sore.

After the dance, the servant wanted to hear about Alice's adventures. Alice told them everything. She told them about the white rabbit and the mouse and the Duchess. The Mock Turtle and the servant agreed that Alice's day had been very strange.

The Mock Turtle liked to sing, so when Alice had finished her stories, he started to sing a sad song called "Turtle Soup".

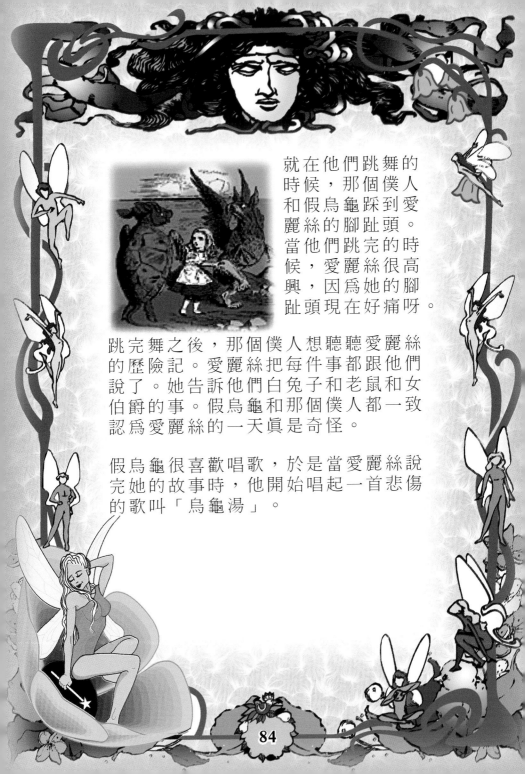

就在他們跳舞的時候，那個僕人和假烏龜踩到愛麗絲的腳趾頭。當他們跳完的時候，愛麗絲很高興，因為她的腳趾頭現在好痛呀。

跳完舞之後，那個僕人想聽聽愛麗絲的歷險記。愛麗絲把每件事都跟他們說了。她告訴他們白兔子和老鼠和女伯爵的事。假烏龜和那個僕人都一致認為愛麗絲的一天真是奇怪。

假烏龜很喜歡唱歌，於是當愛麗絲說完她的故事時，他開始唱起一首悲傷的歌叫「烏龜湯」。

However, in the middle of the song they all heard shouting. The Mock Turtle stopped singing. They listened and again they heard shouting. Someone was saying "the trial is beginning!" The servant took Alice's hand and ran towards the voice. Alice wanted to know about the trial, but the servant continued to run very quickly.

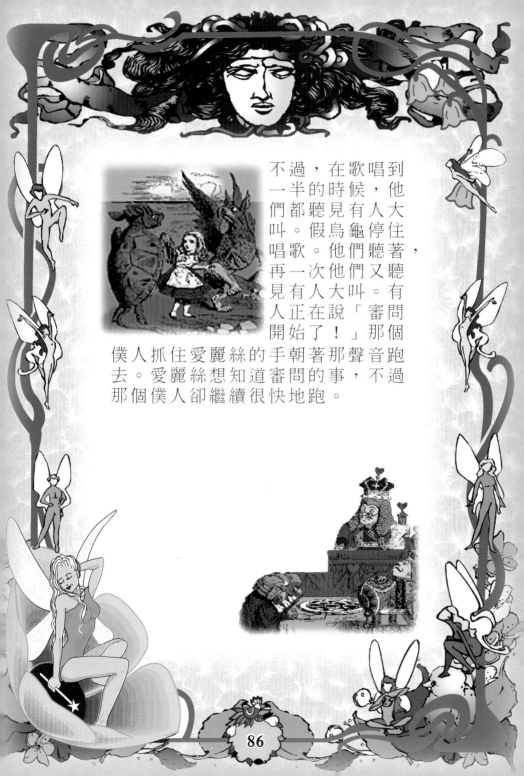

不過，在歌唱到一半的時候，他們都聽見有人大叫。假烏龜停住唱歌。他們聽著，再一次他們又聽見有人大叫。有人正在說「審問開始了！」那個僕人抓住愛麗絲的手朝著那聲音跑去。愛麗絲想知道審問的事，不過那個僕人卻繼續很快地跑。

ALICE BECOMES INVOLVED IN THE TRIAL OF THE KNAVE

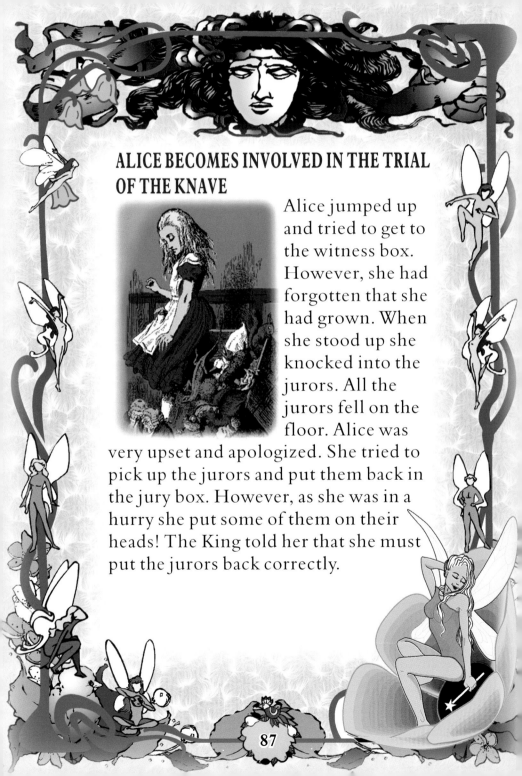

Alice jumped up and tried to get to the witness box. However, she had forgotten that she had grown. When she stood up she knocked into the jurors. All the jurors fell on the floor. Alice was very upset and apologized. She tried to pick up the jurors and put them back in the jury box. However, as she was in a hurry she put some of them on their heads! The King told her that she must put the jurors back correctly.

愛麗絲捲入騙子的審問中

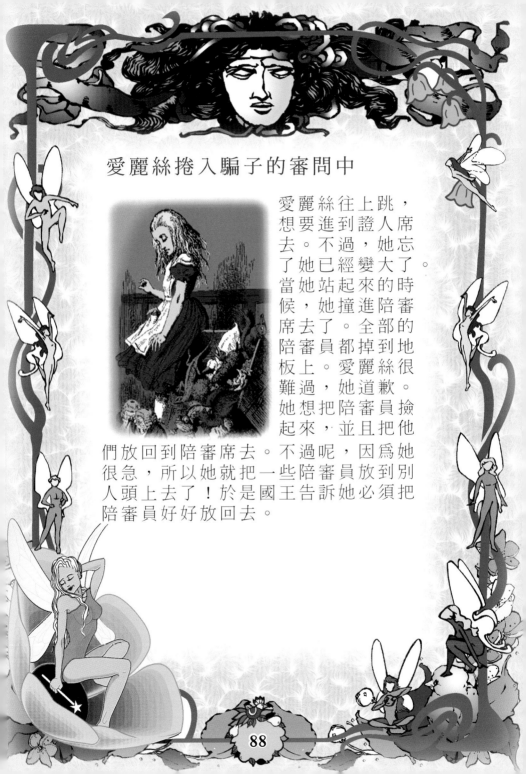

愛麗絲往上跳，想要進到證人席去。不過，她忘了她已經變大了。當她站起來的時候，她撞進陪審席去了。全部的陪審員都掉到地板上。愛麗絲很難過，她道歉。她想把陪審員撿起來，並且把他們放回到陪審席去。不過呢，因為她很急，所以她就把一些陪審員放到別人頭上去了！於是國王告訴她必須把陪審員好好放回去。

As soon as everything was in order the King asked Alice what she knew about the tarts. Alice told the King that she knew nothing about the Knave or about the tarts. The King then looked in his book. He told Alice that there was a special rule. The rule said that people over one mile high could not be at the trial. Alice said that she was not over one mile high. She thought that the king was lying.

一當所有的事情都上軌道時，國王就問愛麗絲說她知道關於蛋塔的什麼事嗎。愛麗絲告訴國王說她不知道什麼關於騙子和蛋塔的事。然後國王就看著他的書。他告訴愛麗絲說有一條特殊的法律。那條法律說凡是身高超過一英哩的人，不可以參加審問。愛麗絲說她並沒有超過一英哩高呀。她認爲國王在撒謊。

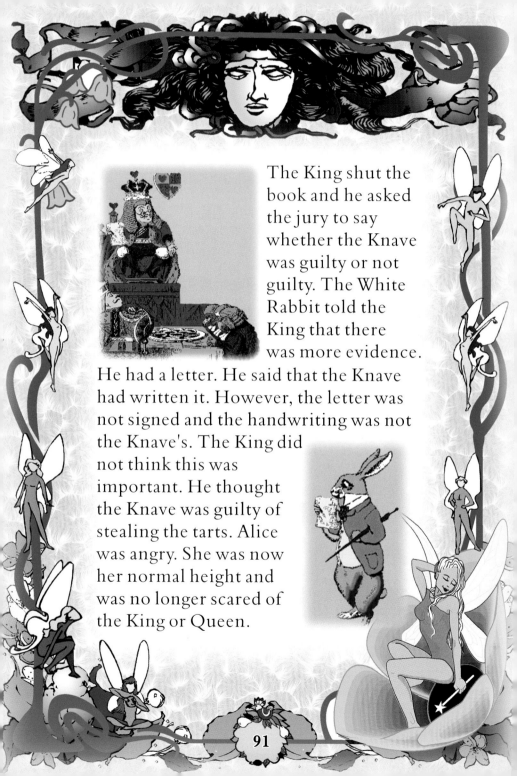

The King shut the book and he asked the jury to say whether the Knave was guilty or not guilty. The White Rabbit told the King that there was more evidence. He had a letter. He said that the Knave had written it. However, the letter was not signed and the handwriting was not the Knave's. The King did not think this was important. He thought the Knave was guilty of stealing the tarts. Alice was angry. She was now her normal height and was no longer scared of the King or Queen.

國王把書閣上，然後他叫陪審團說那個騙子有罪還是無罪。白兔子告訴國王說有更多的證據。他有一封信。他說那個騙子寫了這封信。不過呢，這封信沒有簽名，而字跡也不是那個騙子的。國王不認為這是重要的。他認為那個騙子有罪，因為他偷了蛋塔。愛麗絲很生氣。她現在是她的正常身高，再也不怕國王或皇后了。

She told the courtroom that the letter could not be used.

The Queen was in a hurry. She also wanted the jurors to say that the Knave was guilty. She told Alice to be quiet. When Alice disagreed the Queen shouted "off with her head!" Alice told the courtroom that she did not care and she thought that everyone was very silly.

On hearing this all the creatures stood up and ran towards Alice. Alice screamed and tried to beat them off.

她跟法庭說不可
以用那封信。

皇后很急。她也
想要陪審團說那
個騙子有罪。她
叫愛麗絲安靜。
當愛麗絲不肯時，
皇后便大叫「把
她的頭砍了！」愛麗絲告訴法庭說她
不在乎，而且她認為大家都很愚蠢。

一聽到這個，所有的動物都站起來，
同時跑向愛麗絲。愛麗絲尖聲大叫，
想要把他們打退。

Alice woke up and found she was lying on the bank of the river. She had leaves on her face and her sister was moving them. Alice was very surprised. She told her sister that she had been dreaming. It was a very strange dream. Alice's sister thought that the dream was very exciting. However, it was late. She told Alice to go home for her tea.

愛麗絲醒過來，發現她躺在河邊。她的臉上有樹葉，而她的姊姊正在把葉子拿掉。愛麗絲很驚訝。她告訴她姊姊她做了一個夢。是一個很奇怪的夢。愛麗絲的姊姊認爲那個夢很有意思。不過，時間已經很晚了。她叫愛麗絲回家去喝茶。

After Alice had left, her sister closed her eyes and thought about Alice's dream. She almost believed that she was also in Wonderland. She thought about the white rabbit and the mouse. She could hear the Queen's voice saying "off with her head!". She thought about the sad Mock Turtle and his stories.

在愛麗絲離去之後，她的姊姊閉上眼睛，想著愛麗絲的夢。她幾乎就要相信她也在仙境裡。她想著那隻白兔子和那隻老鼠。她聽得到那皇后的聲音說著「把她的頭砍掉！」她想著那隻傷心的假烏龜和他的故事。

Lastly she thought about Alice. She imagined Alice when she was grown up. She saw Alice and her children. The children would be listening to Alice's stories of Wonderland and they would be as excited as Alice and her sister.

想著麗絲。

她以後愛麗絲，她想愛麗絲像長大子。之後她想見她絲的看著麗絲和她的小孩。那些小孩會聽著愛麗絲夢遊仙境的故事，而且他們也會像愛麗絲和她的姊姊一樣高興。

國家圖書館出版品預行編目資料

愛麗絲夢遊仙境 = Alice's adventures in
Wonderland / Lewis Carroll原著；Anne
Suzane改編. -- 臺北縣五股鄉：萬人，2002
〔民91〕
　　面；　公分. -- （看世界文學名著學英文
：3）（世界文學名著精選：3）
中英對照
ISBN 957-461-064-0(平裝). -- ISBN 957-
461-065-9(平裝附光碟片)

　　1.英國語言 - 讀本

805.18　　　　　　　　　　　　91006782

看世界文學名著學英文 3

愛麗絲夢遊仙境

原　　著/ *Howard Pyle*
改　　編/ **Anne Suzane**

藝術總監/ 霍仲義
美術編輯/ 莊紋芳

發 行 者/ 謝長庚
出 版 者/ 萬人出版社有限公司
地　　址/ 台北縣五股工業區五權七路68號3樓
電　　話/ **(02) 22980501**

總代理:時報文化出版
電　話:02-23066842
日　期:2017年5月
特　價:書+1CD+CD-R 250元